Spreading Sprinkles

Ambie, I ♥ you!
Kelsey

Written by Kelsey Kennedy & Drawings by Brad Dinsmore

Mrs. Donut came out of the oven fresh and abundant with sprinkles. As she looked at herself for the first time she smiled. She knew nobody would be able to resist her hot pink treats.

"Everything is better with sprinkles on top! Oh, what happiness these sprinkles will bring to those that receive them!" she cheered with delight.

Then off she went to share the little pieces of herself.

On the first steps of her journey, she
noticed she was already leaving a trail.
These sprinkles are delicate to the touch,
she thought to herself.

Mrs. Donut decided then and there that she would be intentional in how she shared them.

"I will be thoughtful, but generous. With each sprinkle I share, I give you a piece of my heart!" she shouted joyfully for all to hear.

Whenever Mrs. Donut noticed others in need, she shared a few extra sprinkles. Seeing the sparkling effect they had on others brought joy to her heart.

Constantly scattering sprinkles with each
moment in time, she was filled with purpose.
She knew that her loss and her actions were
making others a little bit brighter. "There's
nothing these sprinkles can't do!" she cried.

She didn't bother to give attention to the slowly dropping sprinkles. Little pieces of herself were here and there. And although she failed to notice, those that got just a small taste of her sweetness never forgot her gift.

Sometimes others took more sprinkles than they realized. "Ouch!" she'd holler, "That hurt me a little!" She was always surprised at how quickly her sprinkles could go.

Mrs. Donut began to notice she wasn't quite as sparkly as she once was. Knowing that in a short time she would have none left, she said, "I must enjoy these last moments."

And with that, she began to dance.
"Shake those sprinkles! "Mrs. Donut
sang.

Her loved ones wept as her last sprinkle fell.

Then suddenly, something magical happened. As they looked back at her trail of sprinkles, they began to feel joy. "But wait!" they shouted, "That's what a donut was made for! Sprinkles are meant to be spread!" They had all had a taste of Mrs. Donut, and those sprinkles had become a part of them.

They looked down at their own uniquely glazed and delightfully sprinkled bodies, they now understood the power of spreading sprinkles.